Moony B. Finch,
the Fastest Draw in the West

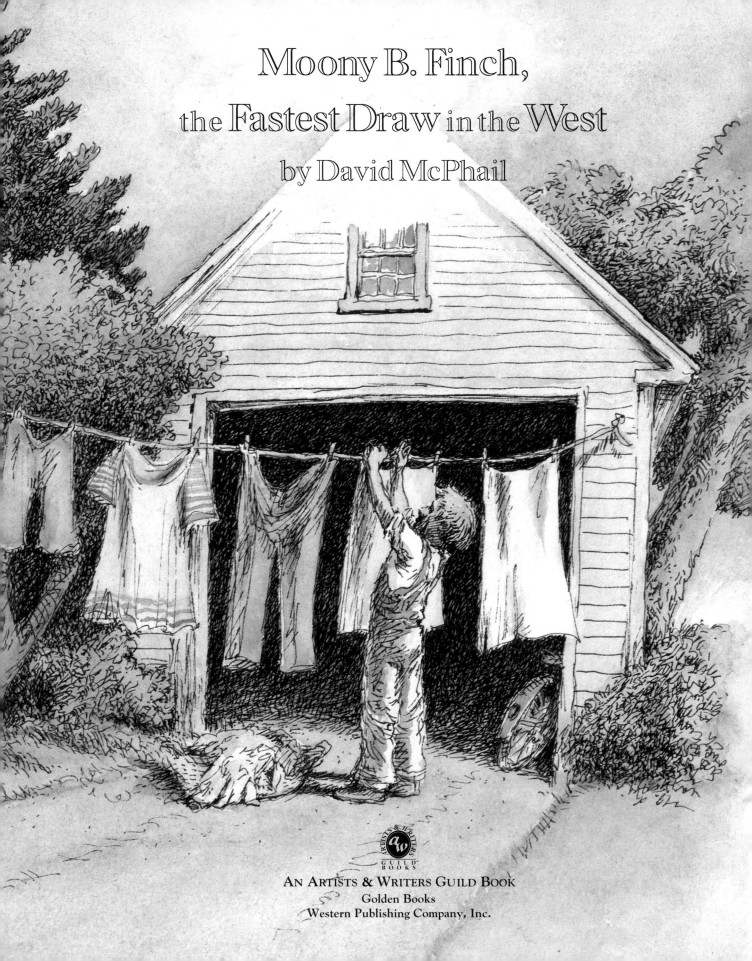

Moony B. Finch,
the Fastest Draw in the West
by David McPhail

AN ARTISTS & WRITERS GUILD BOOK
Golden Books
Western Publishing Company, Inc.

For the Mighty Renster, a worthy opponent.

Library of Congress Cataloging-in-Publication Data

McPhail, David M.
Moony B. Finch, the Fastest Draw in the West/by David McPhail.
p.   cm.
Summary: One quiet spring morning, a young boy uses his magic
pencil to draw an old-fashioned passenger train and then finds
himself among an odd assortment of passengers in the middle of a
train robbery.
ISBN: 0-307-17554-5 (lib. bdg.): $12.95
[1. Drawing—Fiction. 2. Magic—Fiction. 3. Railroads—
Trains—Fiction. 4. Robbers and outlaws—Fiction.] I. Title.
PZ7.M4788184Mo 1994
[E]--dc20   93-37408
                                              CIP
                                              AC

Moony B. Finch loved to draw. He could draw so well that sometimes what he drew became real.

Moony might draw a kangaroo. Then he would lay
his hand on the drawing and the kangaroo would jump
right off the page.

If he wanted to make the kangaroo disappear, Moony
would draw it again. Then he'd take his just-in-case eraser
and erase the new drawing. As he did so, the kangaroo would
vanish . . . line by line, stroke by stroke.

One beautiful spring day Moony tucked his drawing pad under his arm and set out along the abandoned railroad track that ran behind his house.

When he reached the boarded-up railroad station, Moony thought about how exciting it would be if an entire train suddenly appeared.

He sat down on the platform and imagined what an old passenger train would look like. Then he drew it. When Mooney was finished, he laid his hand on the picture.

Suddenly, the earth trembled beneath Moony's feet and then the screech of a train whistle pierced the air.

Above it Moony could hear the voice of the conductor calling, "All aboard!"

Moony didn't hesitate. He stuffed his pencil and eraser into his pocket and jumped on board the departing train.

"Ticket, please," demanded the conductor as soon as Moony sat down.

Moony didn't have a ticket, but he drew one and handed it to the waiting conductor.

Soon the train was racing through the countryside, streaking past cow-filled fields and big red barns brimming with hay.

Moony looked around the compartment at his fellow passengers. Sitting opposite him was a well-dressed pig who was dropping coins into a large satchel.

Behind the pig, two hen sisters were singing a song in perfect harmony—and across from them a family of raccoons was squabbling over an ear of corn.

Alone at the back of the car, a sleeping cowboy lay
sprawled across two seats.

The train had left the
town far behind and was
racing through the countryside
when—without warning—there
was a terrible screeching of brakes
and the train lurched to a halt!
"Don't anybody move!" shouted
the cowboy. He was waving
a huge pistol in the air.
"Hand over all your
valuables!" he
demanded. He
took off his hat
and held it out.
"Drop everything
in here!"

The two hen sisters had nothing to give, so they spit into the robber's hat.

The raccoons dropped in their buttery half-eaten ear of corn.

"Yuck!" cried the robber. "You'll get my hat all greasy!"

But it was too late. A large and spreading grease spot appeared in the bottom of the hat.

The well-dressed pig squealed and whined, but when the robber pressed the pistol to his nose, the pig dumped the contents of his satchel into the hat.

Next it was Moony's turn. "I don't have anything valuable," he explained.

"Empty out your pockets!" snapped the robber.

Moony did as he was told.

"What are those things for?" asked the robber, pointing to the pencil and the eraser.

"I use them to draw pictures," replied Moony.

"Then draw
a picture of me!"
said the robber.
"All right," said
Moony. "Hold still!"
Moony took
his pencil and, with
a few deft strokes, he
drew a perfect likeness
of the robber.
"Why, it looks just like him,"
remarked the pig.
"Yes, *ugly,*" the raccoons agreed.
"Not ugly enough," clucked the
sisters. While this debate was going on,
Moony picked up his eraser and began to erase.

First the gun.

"Hey! Where'd my gun go?" yelled the robber.

"It was only a cap pistol, anyway," said the pig with a sneer.

Then Moony erased the hat, and all the valuables that the robber had collected fell to the floor.

During the wild scramble for the coins and the other booty, Moony continued to erase.

Suddenly everyone started laughing.

"Look!" howled the raccoons, pointing at the robber.
"He doesn't have any pants!"
The robber stood up and looked down.
Sure enough, his pants were gone.

The robber let out a shriek and dashed for the door, running right into the arms of the conductor.

"I've got you now, Wild Willie," said the conductor. "You won't be robbing any more trains for a long time!"

Moony decided it was time for him to go home. He walked to the door and jumped off the train, just as it began to move again.

Then Moony sat down in the warm grass beside the track and watched the train chug away. He made one more drawing.

Moony drew his house and his yard, with the laundry fluttering in the gentle breeze.

He drew his mother and father, sitting on the back step.

Finally Moony drew himself, sitting between his mother and father.

Then he stopped drawing and touched the paper.